MW00897398

Lisa C. Olson

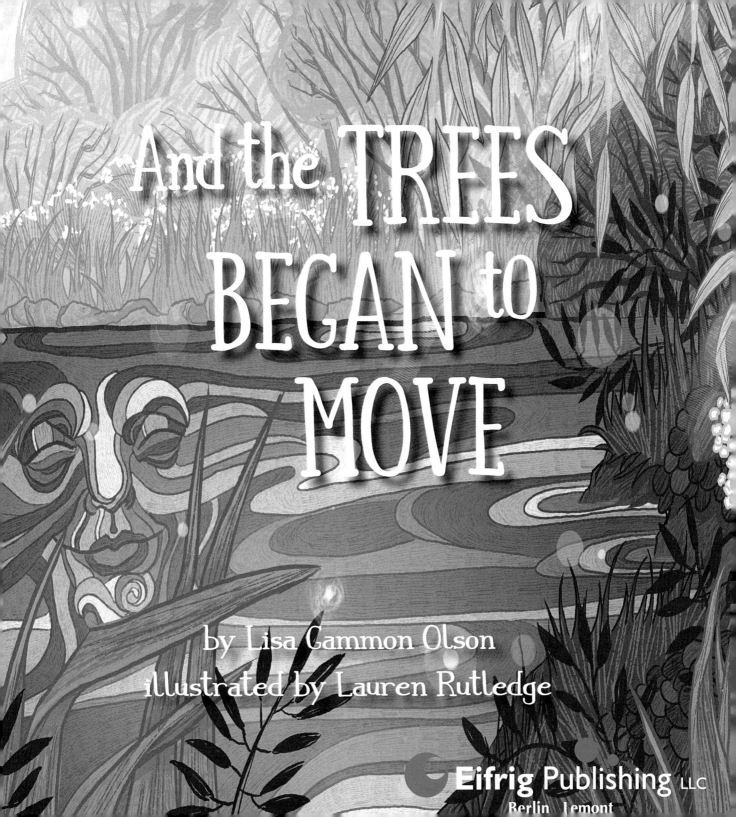

And the TREES BEGAN to MOVE

by Lisa Gammon Olson

illustrated by Lauren Rutledge

Eifrig Publishing LLC

Berlin Lemont

At Eifrig Publishing, our motto is our mission —
"Good for our kids, good for our Earth, and good for our communities."
We are passionate about helping kids develop into caring, creative, thoughtful individuals who possess positive self-images, celebrate differences, and practice inclusion. Our books promote social and environmental consciousness and empower children as they grow in their communities.
www.eifrigpublishing.com

I dedicate this book to my sons, Grant, Kyle & Jay.
You've been a constant source of joy, love & pride in my life.
You ARE and ALWAYS will be My Best Work!
L.G.O.

To Mom and Oscar, whose constant support and encouragement I cannot do without. Thank you!
L.R.

Also by Lisa Gammon Olson
Tales from American HerStory Series:
Dust Flowers
Sewing the Magic in at the Ringling Bros. and Barnum & Bailey Circus
The Cheese Song: All Aboard the Orphan Train
Remembering Green: Introducing Wenonah, an Ojibwe Girl and Her Story

© 2019 Lisa Gammon Olson

Printed in the United States of America

Published by Eifrig Publishing,
PO Box 66, Lemont, PA 16851, USA
Knobelsdorffstr. 44, 14059 Berlin, Germany.

For information regarding permission, write to:
Rights and Permissions Department,
Eifrig Publishing, PO Box 66, Lemont, PA 16851, USA.
permissions@eifrigpublishing.com, +1-888-340-6543

Library of Congress Cataloging-in-Publication Data

Olson, Lisa Gammon
And the Trees Began to Move/
by Lisa Gammon Olson, illustrated by Lauren Rutledge
p. cm.

Paperback: ISBN 978-1-63233-202-8
Hard cover :ISBN 978-1-63233-203-5
Ebook: ISBN 978-1-63233-204-2

[1.Sharing - Juvenile Fiction. 2. Community - Juvenile Fiction 3. Earth Day - Juvenile Fiction]

I. Lauren Rutledge , ill. II. Title

23 22 21 20 2019
5 4 3 2 1

Printed on recycled acid-free paper. ∞

The Spirit of the Pond,
a vain and selfish entity,
wants to preserve his beauty by
denying the Ancient Tree Spirits
his life-giving water in a time
of drought. He discovers that
in trying to save himself,
he will lose everything
he holds dear.

Deep within the forest,
the spirits of all
nature once dwelled
in peace and harmony.

The cool deep pool at the center of the woods
was the heart and soul of the forest;
or so the spirit of the pond thought.

The crystal clear water of the pool
shimmered in the sunlight. The branches
of the gnarled willow and stately oak trees
hung out over the water and dappled the
pool with wonderful leafy shadows that
moved gently with the breeze.

Small silver fish
and glistening green
frogs gathered in the
shadowed coolness
near the water's edge.

"I am so beautiful,"
the pond spirit told himself.
"The sun sparkles so brightly off my
surface. It surely must dazzle all who
look upon me."

The spirit of the pond loved the way the trees,
bushes, and wildflowers reflected their
colorful brilliance in his surface.

He marveled how he
could be no color at all yet
appear to be all colors at once,
always changing his reflection
to mirror his surroundings.

Perfection reigned until a drought came and the rain ceased to fall. The spirit of the pond settled down deep in the cool depths to await the storms, which were sure to come. Days turned into weeks. Weeks turned into months, and still no rain fell on the magical forest.

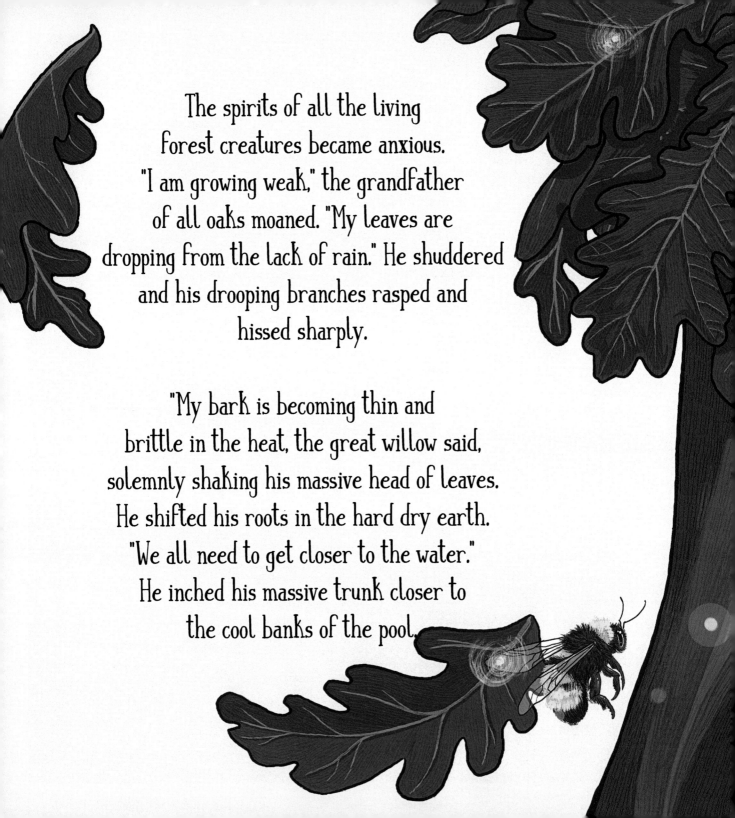

The spirits of all the living
forest creatures became anxious.
"I am growing weak," the grandfather
of all oaks moaned. "My leaves are
dropping from the lack of rain." He shuddered
and his drooping branches rasped and
hissed sharply.

"My bark is becoming thin and
brittle in the heat, the great willow said,
solemnly shaking his massive head of leaves.
He shifted his roots in the hard dry earth.
"We all need to get closer to the water."
He inched his massive trunk closer to
the cool banks of the pool.

The pine trees whispered together in agreement
and with much creaking and cracking they strained to
pull their roots free from the solid ground.

Branches swayed and quivered and leaves rained
down in a dry shower of green as the
ancient trees closed in on the pond.

"Ah," said the mountain ash, as he wriggled his roots deep into the soft muddy bank. "That feels wonderful." "We should have thought of this weeks ago," a honey locust agreed, extending a tendril of root into the healing water of the pond. "I believe I'll have a nice long drink of this cool refreshing water." Grandfather Oak nodded in agreement, and sighs of contentment circled the pond as the great trees quenched their thirst. They drank and drank and drank.

The spirit of the pond awoke from his slumber. Something was different. Something was not right. The surface of the pond didn't twinkle and sparkle above him. The cascading rush of the waterfall was a mere whisper in his ears. What had happened while he slept? He swirled to the surface in a panicky froth of bubbles and foam.

"What catastrophe has befallen us?"
he cried aloud. "Look! The water level
has fallen! Boulders and logs which
were submerged only yesterday are now dry as old bones!"
He ranted and raved as he circled the pond.

"You trees!" he screeched. "You trees are stealing my precious water and blocking the sunlight with your branches. My sparkle is gone! You are too close! The pond lies in shadow and my beautiful colors are dark and stained! You have no right to steal what is mine!"

"We surely meant no harm," Grandfather Oak apologized. "But we will all perish without water, and you have so much to spare."

"I care NOT what happens to you," the pond spirit replied angrily. "I don't help myself to YOUR treasures, do I? Your fruit and seeds are yours to give as you choose, are they not? I will do as I please with what belongs to me."

"We choose to allow those with need to help themselves," the great willow argued. "The birds and squirrels needn't ask for what they need. We are all one in spirit and will share what we have."

"And I will keep what is mine," the pond spirit said coldly. "Now, go!" The trees shook their shaggy heads sadly, but pulled their roots from the moist earth near the pond. The ground trembled and shook as they slowly backed away. "Ah, that's better," the pond spirit whispered to himself as the trees receded and the sun could once again sparkle and dance across his surface.

Another month passed without rain before the spirit of the pond began to worry. With no trees clos to provide shade from the scorching sun, the temperature of the water began to rise.

Warmth-loving algae grew profusely and stained the water with a distinctive emerald tint. The glistening green frogs and small silver fishes that loved to dart in and out of the shadows near the edge of the pond didn't tolerate the changing conditions. The smell of decay was thick.

"I have been very foolish!"
the spirit of the pond cried.
"In trying to save myself, I have indeed
LOST all I hold dear. I have turned my back
on the very ones who have sustained me all these years!"
The brackish water boiled and churned in his anguish.

"Grandfather Oak!" he called. "Mighty Willow!
Forgive my foolish ignorance. I have been vain and very selfish.
Bring your brothers and sisters back to the pond and
I will gladly share my treasures with you!
I will nourish and restore you and
in exchange will restore myself!
For without each other,
we are nothing!"

Silence greeted his plea. He heaved a mighty sigh and prepared to sink down into the murky depths to await his self-inflicted doom.

The water rippled softly once and then again.
The spirit heard a muffled "crack crack."
The earth vibrated ever so faintly at first.
Then the sounds grew ever louder ~ ever closer.
His heart soared!

Grandfather Oak HAD heard.
"SNAP! THUD! CRICK! CRACK!"

The clearing around the pool exploded with
sound as the trees began to move.

And as the last tree returned to its rightful place
near the pond, the magic was restored,
and they could once again live together
in peace and harmony.

In the
Circle of Life,
we are all dependent upon
the actions and kindness
of others. Together we
thrive.

Also by Lisa Gammon Olson:
Tales from American HerStory Series

Exploring tidbits of American history
from the vantage point of a girl protagonist.

Dust Flowers

(Dust Bowl Era)

Sewing the Magic in

(Circus History)

The Cheese Song

(Orphan Trains)

Forthcoming:
Remembering Green
(An Ojibwe Girl's Story)